Tea Leaves

By Frederick Lipp

Illustrated by Lester Coloma

MONDO

To my granddaughter, Ana,
who brings brightness and clarity like sunshine on the sea,
and Jeri Krogh Sides, a muse for writing and being.
—F. L.

To my mom and dad:
Through your courage to cross the ocean and your dedication
to having a better life you have made everything possible.
Thank you for your continuous love and support.
—L. C.

For information contact:

MONDO Publishing

980 Avenue of the Americas

New York, NY 10018

Visit our web site at http://www.mondopub.com

Printed in China

03 04 05 06 07 08 09 10 HC 9 8 7 6 5 4 3 2 1

03 04 05 06 07 08 09 10 PB 9 8 7 6 5 4 3 2 1

ISBN 1-59034-998-9 (hardcover)   ISBN 1-59034-999-7 (pbk.)

Designed by Martha Rago

Library of Congress Cataloging-in-Publication Data

Lipp, Frederick.

Tea Leaves / by Frederick Lipp ; illustrated by Lester Coloma.

p. cm.

Summary: Nine-year-old Shanti, who lives in the mountains of Sri Lanka, has her
wish come true when her Uncle Nochi takes her to see the Indian Ocean.

ISBN 1-59034-998-9 – ISBN 1-59034-999-7 (pbk. : alk.paper)

[1. Sri Lanka--Fiction 2. Indian Ocean--Fiction.] I. Coloma, Lester, 1971-ill. II. Title.

PZ7.L6645Te 2003   [E]--dc21   2003046425

Five minutes into her walk to school, Shanti turned on her heels and ran home.

"Amma, Amma," she cried to her mother.

"Amma, you forgot to wish me good luck."

Shanti smoothed her dark hands over her white school skirt. She straightened her red tie and knelt at her mother's bare feet. With hands pressed together she touched her mother's toes with the tips of her fingers.

"Amma, please give me your wishes for today."

"I wish you good luck, and may you be surprised by what you learn in school," Amma said.

Shanti ran to school and found her class sitting in a circle in the shade of the coconut trees.

Shanti's teacher pressed a pink shell next to her ear.

"Today, we shall learn about the call of the sea. Some people say if you hold a shell to your ear, you can hear the sea," she explained. The teacher passed the shell around the circle. When Shanti pressed the shell to her ear, she heard a soft whisper—like wind in the trees.

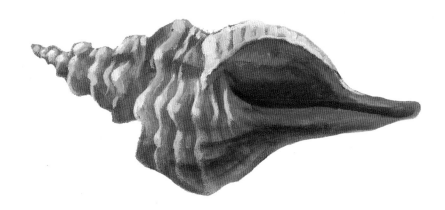

"Raise your hand if you have ever seen the sea," her teacher said.

Whenever she didn't have an answer, Shanti sat on her hands. Slowly, she turned her head and saw that no one in her class had raised a hand.

"But why haven't we seen the sea?" she thought. Shanti knew she lived in the mountains on an island called Sri Lanka. Every tea leaf her mother picked was sent down the mountain.

After school Shanti stood at the edge of the tea garden. She waited until her mother's basket was nearly full before pushing into the thick tea bushes. Little twigs tore at her school dress and snapped at her arms and legs, biting the way red ants did.

"Shanti, I'm working. What are you doing here?"

"I have a question," Shanti said.

The wicker basket was heavy, and Shanti's mother was tired after a hot day of picking leaves. She gripped Shanti by her waist, lifting her slowly above the bushes. They looked over the tea garden spreading down the mountains to where blue sky met the green valley. Shanti asked her question bit by bit.

"Amma, where do the tea leaves in your basket go?"

"Go? Why, they're sent in ships across the sea to England and other places," Amma explained.

"What's the sea?" Shanti continued.

"The sea . . . the sea is all around our mountains. I haven't seen it, but I've heard stories about it."

"Tell me a story." Shanti turned and looked into her mother's dark eyes.

"I have heard stories from Uncle Nochi. He takes our tea in a train from the mountains to ships that sail the ocean. Uncle Nochi told me that the Indian Ocean is filled with so much salt you couldn't drink it. There's salt water as far as you can see. Uncle Nochi told me that on calm days the sea is flat like the palm of your hand, but when there's a storm, waves grow as big as our mountains."

The next morning, Shanti ran to the train station. When the train came for another load of tea, Shanti found Uncle Nochi. He was a tall man with hair as white as clouds.

"Amma says you told her stories about the sea. Will you tell me stories?" Shanti pleaded.

"Hah, the best stories are ones you know yourself," Uncle Nochi said. "You must go to the Indian Ocean. Splash in the water. Build a sand castle that comes up to your nose. Taste the salt. See with your own eyes the waves that go on and on.... I'll tell you what. If your Amma sends me a note and a little money, then I'll take you in my diesel engine to a town by the sea."

When Amma returned home after work, Shanti told her about the visit with Uncle Nochi and his invitation. Amma clicked her tongue when she was angry.

Click . . . click.

"I could never wish you good luck if you go to the sea. Why leave home? We have everything we need in the mountains.

Rice and curry.

Coconut milk.

Bananas.

Your school is down the road."

Click . . . click, click.

"Besides, Shanti, I don't have the money. It took me days of picking tea leaves so you could have a white skirt and blouse for school. For only a few rupees, I pick two leaves and a bud, two leaves and a bud. ALL DAY LONG!"

Shanti grew quiet. She remembered how little money there was to buy a bowl of rice.

"Maybe one day I'll see the sea . . . ," Shanti whispered.

"Maybe," Amma said.

Amma stared out the window. She stopped clicking her tongue. She thought a long time and said, "I'll think about the trip in my dreams."

But even on full-moon nights when Shanti believed dreams could come true, nothing happened.

Then one dark night when she couldn't see the moon at all, Shanti grew so tired of waiting, she went to bed early. She dreamed that the moon decided never to shine across the sea again, because no one ever came to visit its vast waters. With a great swoosh, the full moon blew out like a candle. In her dream, all the oceans became so lonely at night without moonbeams that they dried up. Piles of salt as tall as castles were everywhere.

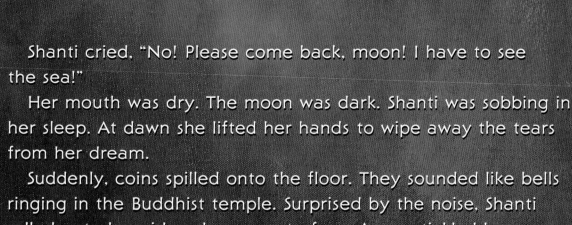

Shanti cried, "No! Please come back, moon! I have to see the sea!"

Her mouth was dry. The moon was dark. Shanti was sobbing in her sleep. At dawn she lifted her hands to wipe away the tears from her dream.

Suddenly, coins spilled onto the floor. They sounded like bells ringing in the Buddhist temple. Surprised by the noise, Shanti rolled onto her side, where a note from Amma tickled her nose.

"On the darkest night my dream came true," she thought. "Now, I can go with Uncle Nochi."

After Amma gave Shanti a bowl of rice and curry, Shanti dressed in her white school skirt and white blouse and red tie. "This is my learning day," she thought. She knelt at her mother's toes.

"Amma, please give me your wishes."

"I wish you good luck, and may you learn from the sea."

Shanti ran to the train station. Uncle Nochi lifted her into the diesel engine. He read her mother's note carefully and put the coins in his pocket. Uncle Nochi pulled a chain, making the whistle echo through the mountain valley.

"Indian Ocean, here we come . . . ," Uncle Nochi sang over and over.

Shanti looked through the black smoke rising from the stack.

Shanti, on tiptoes, looked out the open window as the train descended the mountain with its brakes screeching. It moved down the narrow track just the way a caterpillar crawls down a eucalyptus branch.

A heavy mist rose from the valley. As the train rolled down the track, the day grew hotter. Shanti had not, in all her nine years, been this hot. The fiery blast of the engine and the jungle heat washed her body with sweat.

"Close your eyes now," said Uncle Nochi. The train moved past broken-down trains and buildings.

"Open your eyes, Shanti. There's the Indian Ocean," Uncle
Nochi said proudly, pointing out the window.
    The train moved past buildings crowded with people.
The track ran along the seaside. Shanti forgot the heavy heat
and the salty sweat stinging her eyes. Cows and dogs moved
out of the way of the train. Shanti watched the little fishing
boats riding the waves.

After the tea boxes were unloaded, Uncle Nochi and Shanti jumped in a tuk-tuk and rode down the twisting streets, around people, and between buildings. Suddenly, she saw a great, great bowl of water. The blue spread out in all directions, as far as her eyes could see.

At first, Shanti walked slowly. Then with each step she moved faster and faster until she was running full speed into little waves that met the beach. She folded her hands together to make a cup and dipped her cupped hands into the great sea. She poured the salt water over her head.

Cooling droplets salted her lips. Shanti danced. She jumped up and down in the sea. Once, a wave tipped her over. She drank a whole mouthful of water and came up surprised—and a little frightened.

"The sea! The bright blue sea!" she yelled over her shoulder at Uncle Nochi. "How will I tell my Amma what I have seen?"

Shanti found a pink shell. She found a small, clear bottle, and she filled it with water before leaving. Carrying the shell and the little bottle in one hand, Shanti walked with Uncle Nochi back to the train station.

The tea train twisted like a snake slowly back up the mountain. Shanti held her shell and bottle of seawater tightly. She didn't spill a drop.

When she arrived back at the cottage, her mother woke up as soon as Shanti opened the door.

"Oh, Shanti, I worried about you. It's good to have you safe at home. Tell me, what is the sea like?"

Shanti held out the pink shell for her mother. Then she gave her mother the little bottle of seawater.

"Amma, the sea looks like our sky turned upside-down. It's blue as far as you can see . . . and it sounds like the wind before a storm blowing through the tea garden," Shanti said.

"How does the sea smell?" Amma asked.

"It smells a little like the tea when it's dried in the factories . . . and it tastes like salted herbs from our garden," Shanti went on.

"And how does it feel to swim in the sea?"

"The water is as warm as the river where we wash. The waves are strong like the wind."

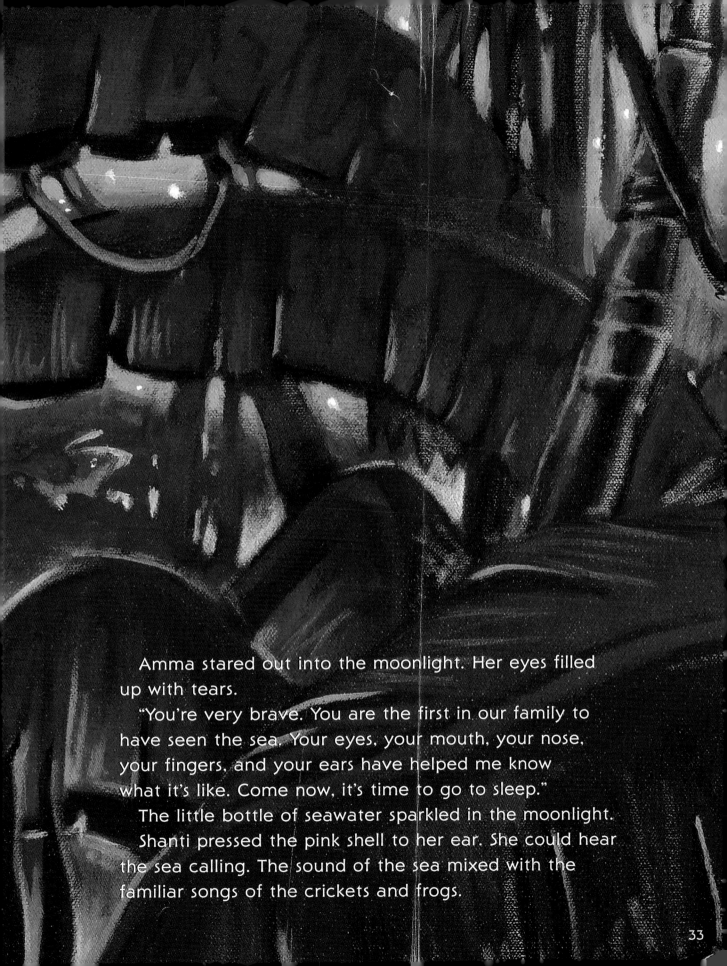

Amma stared out into the moonlight. Her eyes filled
up with tears.

"You're very brave. You are the first in our family to
have seen the sea. Your eyes, your mouth, your nose,
your fingers, and your ears have helped me know
what it's like. Come now, it's time to go to sleep."

The little bottle of seawater sparkled in the moonlight.

Shanti pressed the pink shell to her ear. She could hear
the sea calling. The sound of the sea mixed with the
familiar songs of the crickets and frogs.